Dear Parents and Educators,

Welcome to Penguin Young Readers! As parents and educators, you know that each child develops at his or her own pace—in terms of speech, critical thinking, and, of course, reading. Penguin Young Readers recognizes this fact. As a result, each Penguin Young Readers book is assigned a traditional easy-to-read level (1–4) as well as a Guided Reading Level (A–P). Both of these systems will help you choose the right book for your child. Please refer to the back of each book for specific leveling information. Penguin Young Readers features esteemed authors and illustrators, stories about favorite characters, fascinating nonfiction, and more!

The Pizza That We Made

LEVEL 2

GUIDED READING LEVEL **H**

This book is perfect for a **Progressing Reader** who:
- can figure out unknown words by using picture and context clues;
- can recognize beginning, middle, and ending sounds;
- can make and confirm predictions about what will happen in the text; and
- can distinguish between fiction and nonfiction.

Here are some **activities** you can do during and after reading this book:
- Make Connections: The kids in this story love cooking! Draw pictures of what you like to make in the kitchen. Label all of the ingredients you would use.
- Find the rhyming words in the story. On a separate sheet of paper, write each word next to the word it rhymes with. Use the chart below as an example.

Word	Rhymes with
fine	
tune	
chop	

Remember, sharing the [...] the best gift you can give!

—Bonnie Bader, EdM, and [...] Carella, EdM
  Penguin Young [...]

*Penguin Young Readers are [...] and Gay Su Pinnell in Match[...] [...]veloped by Irene Fountas [...]inemann, 1999.

For Mom and Dave,
two pizza lovers—JH

For Jeff, the great chef—LC

Penguin Young Readers
Published by the Penguin Group
Penguin Group (USA) Inc., 375 Hudson Street, New York, New York 10014, USA
Penguin Group (Canada), 90 Eglinton Avenue East, Suite 700, Toronto,
Ontario M4P 2Y3, Canada (a division of Pearson Penguin Canada Inc.)
Penguin Books Ltd., 80 Strand, London WC2R 0RL, England
Penguin Group Ireland, 25 St. Stephen's Green, Dublin 2, Ireland
(a division of Penguin Books Ltd.)
Penguin Group (Australia), 250 Camberwell Road, Camberwell, Victoria 3124, Australia
(a division of Pearson Australia Group Pty. Ltd.)
Penguin Books India Pvt. Ltd., 11 Community Centre, Panchsheel Park, New Delhi—110 017, India
Penguin Group (NZ), 67 Apollo Drive, Rosedale, Auckland 0632, New Zealand
(a division of Pearson New Zealand Ltd.)
Penguin Books (South Africa) (Pty.) Ltd., 24 Sturdee Avenue, Rosebank,
Johannesburg 2196, South Africa

Penguin Books Ltd., Registered Offices: 80 Strand, London WC2R 0RL, England

Text copyright © 2001 by Joan Holub. Illustrations copyright © 2001 by Lynne Cravath.
All rights reserved. First published in 2001 by Viking and Puffin Books, imprints of
Penguin Group (USA) Inc. Published in 2011 by Penguin Young Readers, an imprint of
Penguin Group USA Inc., 345 Hudson Street, New York, New York 10014.
Manufactured in China.

Library of Congress Control Number: 2001000111

ISBN 978-0-14-230019-0   10 9 8 7 6 5 4 3

PENGUIN YOUNG READERS

LEVEL
PROGRESSING
READER
2

The Pizza That We Made

by Joan Holub
illustrated by Lynne Cravath

Penguin Young Readers
An Imprint of Penguin Group (USA) Inc.

We are the cooks:

Suzanne, Max, and Jake.

This is the pizza

that we will all make.

This is the way
that we begin.
These are the things
that we will add in.

This is the flour,

so soft and fine.

This is the cup

we fill to the line.

This is the mix

we stir with a spoon.

This is the way

we sing a fun tune.

SALT

These are our hands
that mash and fold.

These are our fingers
that push and mold.

This is our bowl.

It's just the right size.

In goes the dough.

It's starting to rise!

This is the way

we make the dough fly.

We toss it down low.

We toss it up high.

This is the dough
we spread in the pan.

This is the sauce
we pour from a can.

These are the green things
we chop, chop, chop.

This is the cheese

that goes on top.

This is the oven

we use to cook.

This is the window.

Let's all take a look!

This is the mess
that we clean away.

We wipe. We sweep.

We're done. Hooray!

This is the way

the table is set.

Where is the pizza?

Is it ready yet?

This is the clock.

There goes the bell.

Sniff. Sniff. Mmmm.

What a great smell!

This is our pizza.

It's ready to eat.

It tastes so yummy.

What a great treat!

These are the crusts
left on each plate.

This *was* the pizza
that we all ate.

Make your own pizza!

(Ask an adult for help using sharp tools or the oven.)

WHAT YOU WILL NEED FOR THE DOUGH:

$2/3$ cup warm water
1 teaspoon active dry yeast
$1/2$ teaspoon sugar
$1/2$ teaspoon salt
1 tablespoon oil (olive oil is best)
$1\,2/3$ cups flour

1. Preheat oven to 400 degrees.
2. Mix yeast and water in a bowl.
3. Stir in sugar, salt, and oil.
4. Slowly mix in flour.
5. Knead dough on a lightly floured, clean surface for 2 minutes.
6. Place dough ball in a bowl and cover. Let it rise in a warm place for 45 minutes.
7. With greased hands, spread dough to fill a lightly oiled 12-inch pizza pan.

WHAT YOU WILL NEED FOR THE TOPPINGS:

$3/4$ cup pizza sauce
1 cup grated mozzarella cheese
Vegetables such as green peppers, tomatoes, broccoli, onions, mushrooms

1. Spread sauce on the dough.
2. Chop vegetables and put them on top of the sauce.
3. Sprinkle cheese over everything.
4. Bake pizza for 15 to 25 minutes or until it looks done.

Enjoy!